This book belongs to:

_____

for Anna and Katy

This paperback edition first published in 2012 by Andersen Press Ltd.
First published in Great Britain in 1998 by Andersen Press Ltd.,
20 Vauxhall Bridge Road, London SW1V 2SA.
Published in Australia by Random House Australia Pty.,
Level 3, 100 Pacific Highway, North Sydney, NSW 2060.
Text copyright © Paul Stewart, 1998.
Illustrations copyright © Chris Riddell, 1998.
The rights of Paul Stewart and Chris Riddell to be identified
as the author and illustrator of this work have been asserted by them
in accordance with the Copyright, Designs and Patents Act, 1988.
All rights reserved. Colour separated in Switzerland
by Photolitho AG, Zürich.
Printed and bound in Singapore by Tien Wah Press.

10   9   8   7   6   5   4   3   2   1

British Library Cataloguing in Publication Data available.

ISBN 978 0 86264 998 2

This book has been printed on acid-free paper

A Little Bit of Winter

Paul Stewart and Chris Riddell

ANDERSEN PRESS

"I'll miss you," said Rabbit. "Will you miss me?"

"No," said Hedgehog.

"I'll miss *you*," said Rabbit.

"I know," said Hedgehog, "you have just told me."

"You are forgetful," said Hedgehog.

"Forgetful?" said Rabbit.

"If you were not," said Hedgehog, "you would remember *why* I will not miss you."

"Remind me," said Rabbit.

"I will be asleep," said Hedgehog. "You do not miss friends when you are asleep."

Hedgehog picked up a little, sharp stone
and walked to the tree.
Rabbit ate a little green grass, and then
a dandelion leaf, and then some clover.
Hedgehog wrote a message on the bark.

"Rabbit," said Hedgehog, "there is something I want you to do for me. It will be hard for an animal who is so full of forget. So I have written a message – to remind you. I want you to save me a little bit of winter."

"But why?" said Rabbit.

"I want to know what winter *feels* like," said Hedgehog.

"Winter is hard and white," said Rabbit.

"Winter is cold."

"But what *is* cold?"

said Hedgehog.

"I am cold now.

Cold and . . .

sle-e-e-e-py."

He yawned.

Rabbit prodded his friend.
"Ouch," he cried.

"Rabbit," said Hedgehog.
"It is time for me to find
somewhere warm to spend
the winter."

Rabbit sucked his paw.
"I'll miss you," he said.

Winter was bad that year. Snow fell. The lake
turned to ice. Rabbit was warm in his burrow,
but he was also hungry.

"That is the trouble with winter,"
said Rabbit, as he hopped outside.
"The colder it is, the more food
I want." He looked around. "And
the colder it is, the less food I find."

There was no green grass.
There was no pink clover.

Rabbit had to make do with brown.

Brown leaves.

Brown bark.

A brown acorn.

When Rabbit saw the words on the tree,
he dropped the acorn in surprise.

The acorn rolled.
It gathered snow.
It turned into a small snowball.

Rabbit read the message.

"Oh dear," he said. "A little bit of *what?*"

The wind blew, icy cold. Rabbit looked down at the snowball, and remembered.

"A little bit of *winter*," he said.

Rabbit rolled the snowball
over the snow.

It grew bigger and bigger.

Rabbit wrapped the snowball
in leaves. "They will keep the
warm out. They will keep the
cold in," said Rabbit.

"Then I shall store it
underground."

Spring came. The sun shone. The snow melted
and the lake turned back to water.
Hedgehog woke up.

"Hedgehog!" said Rabbit.
"Rabbit!" said Hedgehog.

"Oh, Rabbit," said Hedgehog,
"you have eaten *winter*."
"No," said Rabbit. "I ate the bark.
Winter I have saved. It is in my
burrow. I shall fetch it for you."

Hedgehog poked at the soft,
brown ball.

"You told me that winter
was hard and white," he said.

"And cold."

"Just wait," said Rabbit.

He pulled off the leaves,
one by one.

Hedgehog stared at the snowball.
It looked like winter.

Hedgehog sniffed the snowball.
It smelled like winter.

Hedgehog grasped the snowball
in his paws.

"*Ouch*," he cried. "It *bit* me."

"*That*," said Rabbit, "is what
winter feels like."

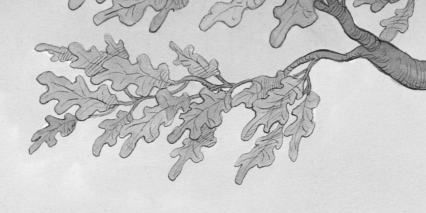

"Thank you for remembering," said Hedgehog.
"I remembered because I missed you,"
said Rabbit. "Did you miss me?"
Hedgehog sighed. "Oh, *Rabbit*," he said.

Also by Paul Stewart and Chris Riddell:

9781842700891

'An enchanting story on the theme of friendship.'

Child Education

Download Rabbit and Hedgehog Me Books
from the App Store!